A catalogue record for this book is available from the British Library

Published by Ladybird Books Ltd
80 Strand London WC2R 0RL
A Penguin Company

4 6 8 10 9 7 5 3

ISBN-13: 978-1-84422-957-4
ISBN-10: 1-84422-957-2

Printed in Italy

Big Digger

written by Jillian Harker
illustrated by Ruth Galloway

On the building site everything is quiet. The builders are sitting in the morning sun, drinking tea and waiting.

Suddenly, a loud rumble shakes the ground. Through the gates at the end of the site comes a huge gleaming yellow machine.
Big Digger has arrived for work.

What a mess! There is plenty of work to do. No building can be done with all of this rubble around.

Big Digger doesn't waste any time. Driver Doug lowers the bucket. Scoop up the rubble, Big Digger! Into the skip it goes.

Next, Big Digger pushes deep down into the ground, making long trenches for the drains. Careful, Big Digger! They have to be in just the right places.

Now for the pipes. Mind they don't fall! Big Digger lowers them down to the builders, to fit end to end. Then the builders can start work on the houses.

The foundations come first.
Is the plan the right way round,
Builder Bill?

Backwards and forwards,
backwards and forwards goes
Big Digger, piling the soil from
the foundations in huge heaps
at the side of the site.

All that digging, and now it has to be filled in again! Big Digger has to carry tonnes of sand to the mixers to make concrete. Fill up the bucket, Doug!

Big Digger lifts the sand high in the air and tips it all out. "Keep it coming!" shout the busy builders.

The next load is a bit heavier. The concrete has set and it's time to start work on the walls. The builders need Big Digger to lift all those bricks. How many are there? One hundred, two hundred, three… well, thousands! There's not enough time to count them all.

It's not long before huge lorries start arriving with wood for roofs and windows. The wood is too heavy for the builders to lift, but not for Big Digger.

"What would we do without you?" they call, as Big Digger raises the roof beams up to the top of the scaffold. Watch out! Has everyone got their hard hats on?

This is looking better! Most of
the houses are nearly ready,
but there is still work to do.
New houses need new roads.
Chug! Chug! Here come the
tipper lorries, loaded high
with hardcore.

Big Digger scoops it up and starts spreading it along the new roadways. They'll soon be ready for the tarmac to be laid on top.

Now there's one final thing to do. The gardens need some good soil. There's a huge pile at the edge of the site that's perfect for the job. But wait a minute – hasn't Big Digger moved all this once before? Never mind! It's fun, building mounds and hills.

What a different site this is now! It's time for Big Digger to head back to the depot.

What's happened to that gleaming yellow machine? Driver Doug knows that Big Digger needs a good wash before they set off again. They're heading out of town to do a very special job at Warner's Farm.

Big Digger arrives at the farm looking as good as new. But not for long! Yuck! What a messy job. When Big Digger has cleared all of that weed out of the pond, the ducks should be happy to get back into it.

So why is Driver Doug laughing?
It might not be that easy! It looks
like the ducks think they have
found a new pond!